PEACHTREE

P9-CQE-967

The Best Place to Read

by **Debbie Bertram & Susan Bloom** ✐ illustrated by **Michael Garland**

Random House 🏠 New York

Text copyright © 2003 by Debbie Bertram and Susan Bloom.
Illustrations copyright © 2003 by Michael Garland.
All rights reserved under International and Pan-American Copyright Conventions.
Published in the United States by Random House Children's Books, a division of Random House, Inc., New York,
and simultaneously in Canada by Random House of Canada Limited, Toronto.

www.randomhouse.com/kids

Library of Congress Cataloging-in-Publication Data
Bertram, Debbie.
The best place to read / by Debbie Bertram and Susan Bloom ; illustrated by Michael Garland.
p.   cm.
SUMMARY: A young child with a new book hunts inside and outside the house before finding the right chair for reading.
ISBN 0-375-82293-3 (trade) — ISBN 0-375-92293-8 (lib. bdg.)
[1. Reading—Fiction. 2. Chairs—Fiction. 3. Mother and child—Fiction. 4. Stories in rhyme.] I. Bloom, Susan.
II. Garland, Michael, 1952– ill. III. Title.
PZ8.3.B4595 Bg 2003
[E]—dc21
2001050099

Printed in the United States of America   First Edition
10 9 8 7 6 5 4 3 2 1
RANDOM HOUSE and colophon are registered trademarks of Random House, Inc.

To Arnie and Jordan,
Our husbands,
our cheerleaders,
our best friends
—With love,
Debbie and Susan

To my aunt Helen
—M.G.

A new book for me—
I can't wait to read!
I run to my own little chair.
I'm growing too tall and the seat is too small,
So I am not comfortable there.

Into the den—
That's a good place to read.
I love Grammy's soft, cozy chair.
But so does old Rover. I tell him, "Move over,"
But he won't make room for me there.

Three eggs.

Daddy's chair must be magic—
The seat can move back, up, and down
In this big leather chair.
A cool, windy feeling—the fan on the ceiling
Is spinning and blasting cold air.

Snack time! I'm hungry—
I'll read in the kitchen.
Baby's booster is next to my chair.
The table's so sticky, my hands get all icky—
YUCK! Why would I want to read there?

Silly bird can fly high.

Grandpa looks comfy
Whenever he reads
In his lumpy and bumpy old chair.
My book drops to my feet when springs poke through
    the seat—BOING!
I bounce up so high in the air.

A nice little worm.

Upstairs! I'll read
In my big brother's room.
I flop on his round beanbag chair.
Surprise! I yell, "EEK!" as the chair springs
    a leak—
There are beans and more beans everywhere.

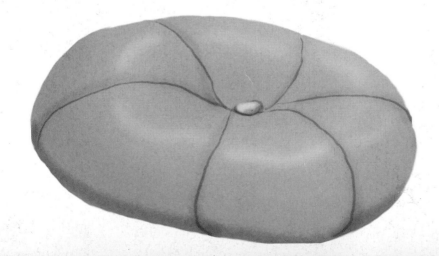

Her Highness, the Princess—
That's my big sis.
A gold seat like a throne is her chair.
But her stereo's singing, her telephone's ringing—
Too loud! Who could ever read there?

Fly high.

So back down the stairs—
Oh, where can I read?
In Auntie's old wood rocking chair.
Like a rocking machine, I feel seasick and green.
I have to go out for some air.

The backyard is great—
I can read on the grass.
I'll sit on a patio chair.
It's the sprinklers—OH, NO!—splashing me head to toe,
So now it's too wet to read there.

I dry myself off.

I give up, I can't read.

I've tried to sit down everywhere.

With no reading done, I'm still on page one—

I *can't* find a comfortable chair!

"Mommy, oh, Mom!
May I sit on your lap?
I love it so much when we share."
The best place to be, just my book, Mom, and me—
At last . . .
In a comfortable chair.

J
PICTURE
BERTRAM

Bertram, Debbie
Best place to read

PEACHTREE
Atlanta-Fulton Public Library